For Meredith

First published 1996 by
Walker Books Ltd, 87 Vauxhall Walk
London SE11 5HJ

2 4 6 8 10 9 7 5 3 1

© 1996 Kim Lewis

This book has been typeset in Bembo Semibold.

Printed in Singapore

British Library Cataloguing in Publication Data
A catalogue record for this book is available
from the British Library.

ISBN 0-7445-4437-8

One Summer Day

Kim Lewis

WALKER BOOKS
AND SUBSIDIARIES
LONDON • BOSTON • SYDNEY

One day Max saw a huge red tractor
with a plough roar by.
"Go out," said Max, racing to find
his shoes and coat and hat.
He hurried back to the window and looked out.

Two boys walked along with fishing-rods.

Max's friend Sara cycled past in the sun.

Max pressed his nose to the window,

but the tractor was gone.

As Max looked out, suddenly Sara looked in.

"Peekaboo!" she said.

Then Max heard a knock at the door.

"Can Max come out?"

"It's a summer day," laughed Sara,
helping Max take off his coat.
The sun was hot and
the grass smelled sweet.
Max and Sara walked down the farm road.

Max and Sara stopped to watch
the hens feeding.

One hen pecked at Max's foot.

"Shoo!" cried Max and sent the hens flapping.

Max and Sara ran through a field
where the grass was very high.
A cow with her calf mooed loudly.
Max made a small "Moo!" back.

Max and Sara
came to the river.
"Look, the boys
are fishing."
Sara caught Max
and took off his
shoes before he
ran in to paddle.

Then Max and Sara reached a gate.

Sara sat Max on top.

They heard a roar in the field

coming nearer and louder.

"Tractor!" shouted Sara and Max.

Max clung to the
gate as the tractor
loomed past.
It pulled a huge
plough which
flashed in the sun.
The field was
full of gulls.

"Let's go home," said Sara to Max.
  They walked beside the freshly plowed field,
  along by the river and through the grass.
  Sara carried Max back up the road.
"Tractor," sighed Max and closed his eyes.

Max woke up when they reached his house.

"Goodbye, Max," said Sara. "See you soon."

Max raced inside to the window.

Sara looked in as Max looked out.

"Peepo!" said Max, and pressed his nose to the glass.